DOCTOR · WHO

DECIDE YOUR DESTINY

BBC CHILDREN'S BOOKS
Published by the Penguin Group
Penguin Books Ltd, 80 Strand, London, WC2R 0RL, England
Penguin Group (USA) Inc., 375 Hudson Street, New York, New York 10014, USA
Penguin Books (Australia) Ltd, 250 Camberwell Road, Camberwell, Victoria 3124, Australia
(A division of Pearson Australia Group Pty Ltd)
Canada, India, New Zealand, South Africa
Published by BBC Children's Books, 2008
This edition produced for The Book People Ltd, Hall Wood Avenue, Haydock, St Helens. WA11 9UL.
Text and design © Children's Character Books, 2008
Written by Jonathan Green
10 9 8 7 6 5 4 3 2 1
ISBN-13: 978-1-85613-159-9
ISBN-10: 1-85613-159-9
Printed in Great Britain by Clays Ltd, St Ives plc

DOCTOR·WHO

DECIDE YOUR DESTINY

The Horror of Howling Hill

By Jonathan Green

The Horror of Howling Hill

1 | Hearing the unexpected hooting of an owl, you suddenly notice how dark the sky has become. Black rags of cloud scud across the darkening velvet blue of night. You had not realised it was so late, and you are still some way from the cottage. The deal was that you could stay out at the playing fields, by yourself, until dusk — then you had to hurry home. But now night has already fallen and you're still nowhere near your holiday house.

You've been there almost a week, enjoying a short country break with the rest of your family on the outskirts of the pretty, chocolate box Wiltshire village of Caernbury. Like Stonehenge and the stone circle at Avebury, Caernbury is steeped in the myth and mysticism of the Stone Age people who used to claim these lands as their tribal hunting grounds.

The owl hoots again, an eerie sound cutting through the night, and you cast your eyes towards the silhouette of the hill away to your left. On its crest, visible against a smattering of stars between the dark shapes of scrubby, wind-blown trees, is the solid black form of the long barrow. The ancient burial mound is one of the local tourist attractions that have put Caernbury on the map. Locally the feature is known as Howling Hill.

It is just at that moment that the owl's screeching cries are silenced by a terrible mournful wail, which echoes around the hillside and over the dreaming village beyond.

You freeze, your blood turning to ice water in your veins. You have never heard anything like it, and you are convinced it came from somewhere nearby. Then the cry comes again, like some unearthly animal wailing, only closer this time. You are not alone.

If you want to run from this place as fast as you can, turn to 45. If you want to stand your ground and see what happens next, turn to 20.

2 Lungs heaving and gasping for breath, you come at last to the local museum which lies at the heart of the village of Caernbury.

It's an unassuming place and unsurprisingly — considering it must be the early hours of the next morning by now — it is all locked up. Peering through the grimy, cobweb-covered windows, you can see nothing: there are no lights on inside.

'What are you waiting for? Christmas?' calls the Doctor from the door to the museum.

Just as you are about to ask how he managed to open the door, he waves the sonic screwdriver at you, as if reading your mind.

Wan moonlight penetrates the dusty windows, bathing the glass display cases and wooden cabinets arrayed around the room with its eerie silvery light.

If Zach Katz is with you, turn to 18.
If not, turn to 72.

3 Unsurprisingly, seeing as how night fell some hours ago, the small museum that stands at the heart of Caernbury, is closed.

You join Martha and the Doctor in peering through the grimy, cobweb-choked windows but can see nothing as there are no lights on inside.

'Oh well, never mind,' you say, trying not to sound too disappointed. 'Time to move on, I guess.'

'Oh, I wouldn't say that,' the Doctor smiles cheekily. 'As an acquaintance of mine once said, where there's a will, there's a way.'

If you want to suggest that you should forget about the museum and push on to the hill, turn to 100. If you want to find out what the Doctor has in mind, turn to 55.

4 'That's simple. It's the cycle. There are reports of attacks and disappearances occurring in the area around Howling Hill every fifty-two years, since there have been records to check. Before that were stories passed on by word of mouth. Every fifty-two years, regular as clockwork.'

'Tricky stuff, clockwork,' muses the Doctor.

'Really?' Zach says, sounding unconvinced. 'I would have thought it would make a change from being chased by laser-toting aliens that want to kill you.'

'Oh, never underestimate the power of clockwork,' the Doctor says darkly.

Zach opens his mouth as if he is about to say something else when that oh-so-familiar dread-filled howl cuts through the still of the night.

Turn to 30.

5 You feel understandably tired after running around Caernbury for half the night, being chased by a monster like something out of some ancient myth, making the climb to the top of Howling Hill and then descending deep inside it.

Easing yourself onto the cold stone of the throne you see that it too is full of tiny glittering seams of crystal. If you didn't know better you could quite easily believe that they looked just like computer circui—

Suddenly your head is filled with unreal images. You see stars streaming past you at hyper-speed, as you hurtle through the blackness of space. Then it is as if you are riding just one of these stars as it drops through the atmosphere towards the night-black landscape below. It looks like you are going to cras—

You come to with a start, feeling Martha's hand on your shoulder.

'W-What was that?' you splutter.

'Are you all right?' she asks for what seems like the umpteenth time.

'I… I don't know,' is your honest reply.

'Interesting,' says the Doctor, peering at you as if you were some kind of experimental subject, like a mouse in a maze. 'I wasn't expecting that.'

Turn to 74.

6 'Quite remarkable,' the Doctor says, half to himself, as he takes a closer look, pen-like device in hand.

'What is it, Doctor?' asks his companion, joining him at his side.

'It's an organic construct, along the lines of a Grendel configuration. Now I haven't seen one of those since around the sixth century AD.'

'And what's an organic construct when it's at home?' Martha persists, drawing the Doctor's attention back to the matter in hand.

'Well, to put it simply, it's a kind of organic robot.'

'Organic? You mean you can just grow your own?' Martha says.

'It's a little more complicated than that, but you've got the gist of it. Only this one appears to be broken.'

'Broken?' you ask, trying to make sense of what you're hearing.

'In other words, it's dead.'

'So this isn't the thing that's been chasing us around this hilltop then?' Martha asks, the colour draining from her cheeks.

'No,' says the Doctor darkly. 'It would appear that there is a second one still active.'

'But who would have an organic robot?' you ask.

'Good question. Let's find out.'

Turn to 41.

7 'Oh yes, a terrible sound, I quite agree,' the Doctor chips in, as you had hoped he would. 'Really sent a shiver down my spine, I don't mind telling you.'

'I can see why they call it Howling Hill,' you add, pointing in the direction of the looming escarpment beyond the village.

'Quite,' Reverend Stukeley says. 'Up until tonight I thought it was only a legend, but having heard the ghastly howling for myself, now I'm not so sure. It would go some way to explaining away all the disappearances that have occurred over the years.'

Disappearances? What disappearances?

If you want to ask about these disappearances, turn to 22. If you would rather ask about the Legend of Howling Hill, turn to 50.

8 You suddenly hear that terrible roar again and the Grendel-beast launches itself out of the darkness of the tunnel ahead of you. With one great swipe of a taloned arm it floors the Doctor, who drops the helmet.

Martha screams but a second swipe from the monster sends her flying too, silencing her cries.

And then it is on you! Snarling, the creature grabs you in its massive hands. The shock is too much for you and, with a feeble cry, you fall into a dead faint...

Turn to 75.

'What's this, the missing link?' Martha asks, peering over your shoulder at the skeleton in the display case as well.

Even to your eyes you can see that the skeleton is a strange shape for a human being. Although it must be about six feet in height, its ribcage and skull seem squashed together, while its arms and legs are long and spindly, its fingertips reaching down past its knees.

'Caernbury Man,' you read from a faded yellow label stuck to the cabinet, 'an example of one of homo sapiens' Cro-Magnon ancestors. Uncovered beneath Caernbury Barrow by Arthur Cornelius Cove, 26th September 1908.'

'Allegedly,' the Doctor snorts. 'If you believe that, you'll believe the Daleks are just a grossly misunderstood peace-loving race.'

What is he talking about now?

'Come on,' he says more chirpily again, 'I think it's time we took a look at this mysterious barrow for ourselves. Allons-y!'

Turn to 100.

'What was that thing?' you ask, as the three of you make your way around the edge of the village, heading towards the church.

'I'm not entirely sure,' the Doctor admits, 'which is precisely why I want to catch up with it — to take a closer look.'

It isn't long before you round a bend in the lane you are following and come upon the lychgate that leads into the graveyard which is attached to the stone-built church. A light shines from beyond the stained glass window at the east end, suggesting that someone is inside. But is this really the sort of place an unearthly seven-foot-tall monster would hide?

If you want to forget about the church and instead suggest that you should make for the hill instead, turn to 100. If you want to press on with your exploration of the church, turn to 29.

11 'Ah yes, Arthur Cove,' the Doctor mutters. 'And that, my friends, is the last piece of the puzzle.'

'Is it?' says Martha, bewildered. 'Then would you mind explaining what's going on around here?'

'All in good time,' the Doctor tells her. 'All in good time. For the time being, it's more important that we get back to the museum as quickly as possible.'

Turn to 26.

12 'Oh, you know, the TARDIS picked up a recurring crystalline pattern energy signal and, well, I guess you could say that our curiosity got the better of us, so here we are!'

'But that's not important right now, is it Doctor?' says the girl, who starts methodically checking you over, as if looking for any bumps or scratches. 'The important thing is, are you okay? I'm Martha, by the way.'

Breathing deeply to calm yourself, your heart-rate returning to something approaching normal, you can't help feeling exhilarated by what has happened to you, as well as a little frightened.

'I'm all right,' you tell her. 'I'll be okay.'

'Great!' says the Doctor. 'Come on then, Martha, time we were on our way. Monster to catch, and all that. Good day to you.'

Turn to 63.

13 The now unpleasantly familiar howl of the beast cuts through the night once again. The creature is still on your trail.

'Yup, definitely a Grendel configuration,' the Doctor says, his head on one side, as if listening intently. 'You can hear it in its vocal matrix once you know what you're listening out for. Anyway, it's time we were on our way again.'

'Doctor, wait!' Martha shouts, bringing you all to a standstill. 'If you know what that thing is now, can't you stop it? You've been able to hold if off so far.'

'I don't think so. Not from here, anyway. The Grendel's relentless. It must be its bio-programming. I'm not sure how long the sonic screwdriver will be able to hold it off either, if it feels determined enough. So, as I was saying, it's time we made our getaway.'

Finding the reserves of energy from somewhere, the three of you race off again, this time down the steep hillside.

'Look!' Martha calls pointing westwards through the night. There at the corner of a field you can see a parked caravan, a satellite dish on its roof, gleaming white in the moonlight. 'Let's go that way!'

'No!' counters the Doctor, pointing east, back towards the village. 'We need to not be distracted. Let's get back to the village.'

'But the caravan's nearer!' declares Martha.

'The village!' the Doctor insists.

Who do you think is right? Whoever you side with, the other will be forced to join you, to avoid the three of you becoming separated.

To follow the Doctor towards Caernbury, turn to 2. To follow Martha in the direction of the caravan, turn to 27.

14 The instant your hand touches the crystal-embedded rock, it begins to pulse with light, which grows in intensity with every pulse.

'What did you do?' presses the Doctor, hurrying over to where you're standing.

'I-I only wanted to see what it felt like,' you stammer, apologetically.

'Oh, don't worry. This is great!' he exclaims excitedly. 'Look at this, Martha!' he calls to his companion. 'I think our young friend may have found the source of the recurring crystalline pattern energy signal the TARDIS picked up.'

'Well done!' Martha says, patting you on the back.

You're quite literally flabbergasted, but can't help yourself beaming at the thought that you may have helped Martha and the Doctor come one step closer to solving the mystery surrounding this strange place.

'Let's keep going,' the Doctor declares, just as excitedly, as he strides out of the chamber into the next one. You trail along after him, grinning from ear to ear.

Turn to 38.

15 You turn to see a short, moon-faced man standing at the other end of the nave, watching the three of you intently from behind round wire-framed glasses. He is wearing plain black trousers and a dull grey cardigan. At his neck is a stark white dog collar.

'I said can I help you?' the vicar asks again.

'Ah, good evening,' the Doctor says, giving the man a broad smile. 'Professor Smith, Professor John Smith. Here with my colleague Miss Jones —'

'Doctor Jones,' Martha corrects him.

'— and one of my students, from the institute.'

'At this time of night?' the vicar challenges, confusion knotting his features.

'And you must be?'

'The Reverend Stukeley.'

'Of course. Of course. Well, we're here as... as...'

'As part of the research team,' Martha butts in.

'Ah, the one looking to excavate the barrow again,' the vicar says, comprehension lighting up his face.

'Yes, that's the one,' the Doctor confirms, grinning wildly.

'Then perhaps I can help,' the reverend offers. 'After all, I am something of an amateur enthusiast when it comes to the Legend of Howling Hill.'

The Doctor shoots a knowing glance your way. Now's your chance to find out more.

If you want to ask the vicar more about the legend, turn to 50. If you want to ask him more about the church's unusual stained glass window, turn to 90.

16 The instant you lift the helmet from your head, a sonorous drone — like the sounding of a carynx horn — fills the chamber. You jump up from the throne as the creature facing you, shudders back into operation, giving voice to its own terrible wail.

You sprint for the tunnel that leads out of the throne room and back up through the hill. Suddenly, there are the Doctor and Martha, at the entrance to the chamber.

'Come on,' he bellows over the rising roar inside the chamber. 'We haven't got much time before the crystal-matrix core engines overload and this whole place blows.'

'What have you done?' you gasp, shocked at his announcement.

'Well, we couldn't have this thing returning to the Omega Nebula with you still onboard, could we?'

Turn to 70.

17 Diving for cover between the two stones that mark the entrance to the mound, you scramble along the damp passageway cut into the earth beyond.

'There you are!' comes Martha's agitated voice from somewhere ahead of you in the darkness. 'Quick, get down!'

Without stopping to ask why, you throw yourself down on the compacted earth floor of the tunnel, glancing back over your shoulder at the small patch of night's sky visible beyond the barrow.

As you watch, your heart in your mouth, you see an even darker silhouette stride past the entrance. It pauses for a moment, looking around, and you hold your breath, fearful that it can hear your heaving breaths. Then the creature raises its head and howls at the moon. A moment later it is gone.

Turn to 28.

18 'Over here,' says Zach, leading you all to the far side of what is effectively just a large room. 'Just look at that,' he says, pointing at a tall display case in which has been mounted a set of bones, 'and tell me that isn't alien.'

'Yes, quite,' says the Doctor, giving the exhibit only a cursory glance before moving on to another display case altogether. This one contains a bronze helmet, set with glittering semi-precious stones.

> **To take a look at the helmet, along with the Doctor, turn to 52. To take a closer look at the skeleton, turn to 37.**

'It really is magnificent, isn't it?' says the Doctor and, before you know it, he's got the cabinet open and he's lifting the helmet from its display stand.

Martha looks around nervously, as if expecting an alarm to go off. 'Breaking and entering, Doctor: are you sure about this?' she asks him.

'Don't worry,' says the Doctor, realising what she must be worried about. 'I deactivated the alarm before we even entered.' Then he turns his attention to the helmet he is now holding in his hands. 'Let's have a look at you, you beauty.'

Activating his sonic screwdriver, the Doctor starts tinkering with the helmet. It is almost as if he is trying to repair it, but as far as you can see, it isn't even broken.

'That's the telepathic command relays realigned and recalibrated,' he says after a few minutes' fiddling. 'Nothing very serious but it would have stopped this little beauty from working as it should.'

'What do you mean, Doctor?' asks Martha, watching him curiously.

'Wait and see,' he says with a smile. 'Now, back to the hill, only this time we're taking this with us.'

'Isn't that stealing?' you can't help but ask.

'I think Arthur Cove was the thief,' says the Doctor, sagely.

There seems to be rather a lot of to-ing and fro-ing with the Doctor, but you're beginning to get an inkling as to what he is up to.

If Zach Katz is with you, turn to 69. If not, turn to 99.

The howling comes again, so close now you can almost believe you can feel the hot breath of some nightmarish, phantasmal creature on the back of your neck. You can see why the escarpment is called Howling Hill!

You try to tell yourself not to be silly. There can't possibly be anything like that out here! You've heard of the Beast of Bodmin, but that's supposed to be some kind of big cat and besides, you're nowhere near Cornwall!

Only you're not imagining things. You really can feel hot gusts of breath on the back of your neck, accompanied by a bullish snorting.

Unable to stop yourself, instinctively you turn round. There before you is a hulking monster like some horror from an ancient legend. It is at least seven feet tall, its lithe, muscular body covered in lank green hair. Thick saliva drips from the yellow tusks cramming its mouth and it studies you from beneath heavily hooded eyes which glow orange, like smouldering coals in the darkness.

The monster opens its mouth again, as if about to roar or swallow you up!

If you want to run from the beast as fast as your legs will carry you, turn to 58. If you want to shout for help with all the breath you have in your lungs, turn to 79.

21 It is incredible to think that whoever made these marks did so thousands of years ago with only the most primitive of tools. Or did they?

As you run your fingers over the time-worn carvings they too begin to glow with an inner light. You pull your hand away in shock and the light fades again.

'Fascinating,' says the Doctor, suddenly at your shoulder. 'What have you found?'

'I-I didn't mean to –' you begin.

'Don't apologise!' the Doctor stops you. 'This is brilliant! I think you might have gone some way to solving the mystery of Howling Hill all by yourself with this discovery!'

At the Doctor's warm words of praise you can't help but feel pleased with yourself, a smile breaking out across your face.

'Come on, let's keep going,' the Doctor declares, as he strides enthusiastically out of the chamber and into the next one. You follow, beaming from ear to ear, as the Doctor leads the way out of the chamber.

Turn to 38.

'There have been a number of disappearances from Caernbury over the years,' the vicar explains as he leads the three of you into the church vestry.

Once there, he opens a musty-smelling cupboard and pulls out a dusty leather-bound tome.

'A predecessor of mine was the first began to record them in the parish records. There's a bit about this recurring mystery at the village museum but the original records are still kept here in the church. They make for fascinating reading.'

'When does the record of these disappearances begin?' the Doctor asks, a pair of thick-rimmed glasses now perched on the end of his nose.

'The first ones date back to 1644. The Reverend Josiah Lister was the one to first chronicle these unexplained disappearances.'

'How many were there?' Martha asks.

'There were four that year,' Reverend Stukeley says, pointing to a handwritten entry in the ledger.

'And they've continued ever since?' the Doctor asks, following the list of dates in the book. 'Every fifty-two years, by the look of things.'

'That's right.'

'Well, thank you for your time, Vicar,' the Doctor says, suddenly bringing the conversation to an abrupt end. 'It's getting late and we really must be on our way.' He gives you a conspiratorial wink.

Once the three of you are in the lane outside the church again Martha asks the Doctor, 'What's the hurry?'

'People have been disappearing from this village every fifty-two years, regular as clockwork, and now it's 2008, if I rightly remember, and our young friend here has just been attacked by the local monster. Time is, as ever, of the essence.'

He shoots you with a wicked grin. 'So, where now?'

If you want to head for hill, turn to 100.
If you want to visit the village museum, turn to 3.

'Doctor!' you call out. 'Throw me the helmet. Zach's got a plan!'

'Well, let's hope it's a good one!' the Doctor calls back as he tosses you the helmet.

You catch it deftly and almost at once see the monster turn away from the Doctor and towards you instead, giving voice to its terrible howling cry.

'There you are,' you say, thrusting the helmet into Zach's hands. 'What are you going to do?'

'Watch,' he says calmly, as he lowers the helmet onto his head.

As the light in the chamber continues to grow in intensity, you see the Grendel-monster freeze. At the same instant, a screen of white light appears impossibly in the air above Zach. Strange blue patterns — not unlike the knotwork carvings that you have seen inside the barrow — start to flicker across the screen, like the letters and words of some alien language. The throbbing hum rises in pitch and intensity.

'It is time you were gone,' Zach says in a strangely distant voice.

'But we can't just leave you here, like this!' you yell over the rising roar of the stone ship's engines.

'Do not worry about me,' Zach reassures you. 'This is what I have always wanted — to see what lies beyond the stars. I'm taking this ship home.'

'What's he doing?' the Doctor asks, suddenly at your side. 'We haven't got time to mess around! We've all got to get out of here right now. Martha, help me with our geeky friend here.'

If you help the Doctor and Martha free Zach from the pull of the ship, turn to 65.
If you try to persuade them to leave him where he is, turn to 78.

24 'You'll find it in the middle of Caernbury,' the vicar tells you. 'You can't miss it.'

'And what might we see there, should we happen to drop by?' enquires the Doctor casually.

'Where there's a fair bit on the flora and fauna of the area but of course the main reason to visit is to see the treasures Arthur Cove recovered from beneath the barrow.'

'Treasure?' Martha chips in, eyes wide in anticipation.

'Priceless artefacts, recovered from inside the hill beneath the barrow,' Reverend Stukeley continues. 'A unique example of a Bronze Age helmet, almost entirely intact, and the bones of Caernbury Man. They really are quite remarkable.'

'Well, thank you for your time, Vicar,' the Doctor suddenly says, abruptly bringing the discussion to an end. 'It's getting late and we really must be on our way.' He gives you a conspiratorial wink.

Once the three of you are in the lane outside the church again Martha asks the Doctor, 'What's the hurry?'

'We've found out all we're going to here,' he explains, and then flashes you a wicked grin. 'So, where now?'

If you say you should head for the hill, turn to 100. If you suggest visiting the village museum, turn to 3.

Finally you find yourselves standing in the shadow of Howling Hill once again. The blustery wind still has that same chilling bite to it that cuts you to the marrow. Your eyes are drawn towards the ominous outline of the burial mound at the top. You know now that it is beneath the barrow where you will help the Doctor and Martha solve the mystery of the Horror of Howling Hill once and for all.

As if right on cue, the mournful wail of the beast echoes from the slopes of the hill. Even now the sound of it still chills you to the bone.

If you have met Zach Katz and he has been abducted, turn to 89. If you have never met Zach Katz, turn to 77.

'I want to come too!' Zach declares, the spark of excitement bright in his eyes.

'Very well,' the Doctor says with a sigh. 'Martha, I make that three against one. Come on!'

Your party now numbering four, with the Doctor leading the way, you all hasten across the field, scramble over a stile and then race off along a country lane back towards the village.

As you run, you still half expect the monster to leap at you again out of the darkness. But no such attack comes and, the Doctor apparently scanning for something with his sonic screwdriver, you come at last to Caernbury's local archaeological museum.

If you have already visited the village museum, turn to 80. If you haven't been there before, turn to 2.

Two against one: the Doctor has no choice but to follow you and Martha in the direction of the curious caravan.

Reaching the edge of the field, the three of you scramble over a five-bar gate and then have to wade through a sucking soup of mud and cow pats to reach the parked vehicle.

'Right then, I'll do the honours, shall I?' says Martha and strides boldly towards the caravan, ready to knock on the door.

If you want to stop her and suggest you should it might be wise to sneak a peek inside the caravan first, turn to 54. If you let her knock on the door, turn to 88.

'That was a bit close for comfort, wasn't it?' comes a chirpy voice from behind you.

'Doctor!' Martha cries, sounding both pleased and cross at the same time. 'What happened to you?'

'You've heard of Alice in Wonderland?' the Doctor says as he emerges from the darkness of the tunnel behind you, his sonic pen-device lighting the way and giving his features a strange blue cast.

'What? Yes, of course. Lewis Carroll,' Martha says, humouring him, an excited gleam in her eye.

'Yes, charming chap. Well, let's just say that I fell into the same rabbit hole as Alice. Come on, this way.'

Too stunned to do anything other, you set off after the Doctor as he leads the way along the damp earth tunnel, deeper into Howling Hill. The tunnel descends the further you progress until you come at last to a junction.

'I would suggest we go,' he pauses, sniffing the air, 'left.'

If you want to go left, turn to 41. If you want to persuade the Doctor to take the right-hand passageway, turn to 101.

'I don't like the look of this place,' Martha confesses as the Doctor leads the way under the lychgate and up the pebbled path towards the open church door.

'Why's that?' you can't help asking.

'Just a hunch.'

'Reminds me of a charming little place I once visited called Devil's End,' the Doctor adds mysteriously.

Then the howl comes again. Closer than before, the blood-curdling cry sends a thrill of fear and excitement coursing through your body. Your heart beats a tattoo of excited anticipation against your ribs.

If you want to seek sanctuary inside the church, turn to 76. If you want to brave it outside and make a search of the graveyard, turn to 39.

30 'Did you hear that?' Zach asks, his voice squeaking with nervous excitement.

'Oh, we heard that all right,' the Doctor replies darkly, 'and it means we're running out of time. The beast is getting close.'

'Come on,' says Zach. 'This is our chance.'

'Our chance to do what?' asks Martha.

'To solve the mystery,' Zach replies, ready to open the caravan door.

'No, we need to get back to the village,' the Doctor persists. 'I'm sure that's where we'll find the next piece of the puzzle.'

'If you say so, Doctor,' Martha concedes, 'but I'm worried about risking our young friend's safety out there with the beast still on the prowl.'

If you think that you should all stay where you are, turn to 86. If you want to convince the Doctor and Martha that you'll be all right outside as long as you're with them, turn 26.

31 You have seen something like this helmet before, only then it was in a history lesson at school and you were learning about the Anglo-Saxon treasures uncovered at Sutton Hoo at the time.

The helmet certainly looks like it could date from that time. It is covered in the fine tracery of wrought knotwork. There are also a number of gemstones set into it which sparkle and shine with refracted moonlight. The object must be worth a king's ransom — priceless, even.

'It takes your breath away, doesn't it,' Martha gasps.

'Come on,' says the Doctor. 'I think we've seen all we need to here. Let's go and take a look at the mysterious barrow where this little lot came from for ourselves, shall we?'

Turn to 100.

32 You push on until you reach the throne room at the heart of the barrow-ship. You stumble to a halt in surprise as you take in what has happened to the vast vault since you were all last here.

Blue light fills the hold beneath the hill, banishing the darkness that has clung on here for so many years. A sonorous sound fills the space as well, just as you would imagine a spaceship's engines would sound if they were powering up ready for take-off.

And there is Zach Katz, slumped in the stone throne. He appears to be unconscious.

Giving voice to a blood-curdling roar, the Grendel-beast launches itself at your party from its hiding place beside the chamber entrance, bearing down on you with loping strides, its terrible talons raised, ready to strike. You scatter into the chamber, the monster pursuing the Doctor. But of course — he has the helmet!

Something tells you the sonic screwdriver isn't going to stop the Horror now so you are going to have to act quickly if you are all going to get out of this in one piece.

If you want to rescue Zach, turn to 82. If you want to help the Doctor, turn to 73.

33 While it is busy retrieving the fallen helmet, finding new reserves of energy from somewhere deep inside, you dash past it and on up the hill heading for the barrow.

But even as you flee, you hear the grunting of the monster as it turns again to pursue you, more determined than ever it seems to hunt you down!

You can hear the creature getting closer with every pounding step. It is only going to be a matter of moments before the thing catches up with you. You are going to have to act fast if you are going to shake it off.

If you want to keep running in the hope of outrunning the monster, turn to 87. If you dare to face it, in the hope of somehow fighting back against it, turn to 64.

34 'I know this probably sounds crazy but I think there's something buried under that hill,' Zach confides in you.

'Like what?' the Doctor asks him bluntly.

'I'm not sure. If it hadn't been for what Arthur Cove's 1908 excavation uncovered I would have said... a spaceship!'

If you have visited Caernbury's village museum, turn to 11. If not, turn to 97.

35 'A horrible haunting sound, it was,' the vicar explains. 'The banshee cry of some demon of the dark.'

Martha catches your eye, raising an eyebrow at the Reverend's flowery language.

'But, if you were out here, you must have heard it too. Well, did you?'

If you want to speak first and answer the vicar, turn to 83. If you want to wait, hoping that the Doctor will answer for all of you, turn to 7.

'No, Doctor,' you say, the time traveller looking suitably taken aback at your refusal to run for it. 'I know what's going on here.'

'You do?' asks Martha, amazed.

'Go on,' encourages the Doctor.

'This spacecraft buried under Howling Hill... It's a Triskele survey ship. It landed here centuries ago but something went wrong and its pilot died.'

'Ah, of course,' says the Doctor excitedly. 'This ship is semi-organic which means there's a psychic link between it and the pilot. Without a pilot the ship was unable to take off again.'

'That's right, and it's been searching for a new one ever since.'

'Let me guess, every fifty-two years the Grendel configuration organic drones are sent out to find a replacement, probably as part of some kind of reserve power cycle. But the command helm, that connects the ship to the pilot, via its psychic relays, was damaged and so whoever the drones brought back, it never worked and so the ship was still stuck here. After Arthur Cove removed it, of course, there was even less chance of the drones succeeding.'

'How do you know all this?' asks Martha.

'The ship spoke to me,' you reply hardly able to believe what you are telling yourself.

'Doctor, you repaired the control helm,' you say earnestly. 'So isn't there something that a man like you could do to save this ship; to send it home?'

The Doctor looks serious for a moment. Then an uncontained grin breaks out on his face.

'I'm sure there is!' he exclaims. 'Should be easy for a man like me!'

With that, he whips out his trusty sonic screwdriver once more and makes some hasty adjustments to the helm before placing it carefully on the throne.

'Now, quick, let's get out of here,' he says as the throbbing hum continues to rise in pitch even more.

'What have you done?' Martha asks him, intrigued.

'Simple. I'm sending it back home on autopilot.'

Turn to 53.

37 The skeleton is a very strange shape for a human being. It is around six feet tall but the ribcage and skull seem squashed together. The arm and leg bones are long and spindly, the skeleton's fingertips reaching down past its knees.

'Caernbury Man,' you read out loud from a faded yellow exhibit label, 'an example of one of homo sapiens' Cro-Magnon ancestors. Uncovered beneath Caernbury Barrow by Arthur Cornelius Cove, 26th September 1908.'

'Looks like the missing link to me,' Martha laughs, 'don't you agree, Doctor? Doctor?'

The Doctor, now wearing a pair of thick-rimmed glasses, is busy studying the Anglo-Saxon helmet in the other display case.

'Never mind that,' he says. 'Come and take a look at this.'

Turn to 52.

38 And so, at last, you come to the last chamber of them all, which also happens to be the largest. The shadowy dome of its roof soars away above you, making it feel like you are standing inside some vast cavern.

The vaulted space is decorated with the same carved stonework, riddled with glittering crystalline deposits. However, where it differs from the other chambers is in the addition of the stone throne. It stands alone, at the centre of the chamber, rising from the bedrock from which it appears to have been carved. But it is empty. The warrior king who must have once slept under this hill is long gone.

As you gaze upon it, you find yourself strangely drawn towards the empty throne.

If you want to rest for a moment and sit on the throne, turn to 5. If not, turn to 74.

The moon casts its eerie light over the graveyard, making you feel even more nervous about your adventurous endeavour.

Creeping between the lichen-scabbed gravestones, your own thumping pulse loud in your ears, you hear the dry snap of a breaking twig.

Martha obviously heard it too. 'Doctor, what was that?' she demands, pulling her leather jacket tight around her.

'Over there!' he hisses, pointing right, and then you catch sight of movement amongst the shadows of the graveyard.

If you want to lead the others back to the church, to escape whatever's out here with you, turn to 76. If you want to stand your ground and confront whatever it is that's stalking the graveyard, turn to 98.

40 You run right round the outside of the barrow, trying to shake off the creature, before heading back to the entrance and ducking inside. You stumble to a halt and peer back towards the opening, in case you can see the monster as it strides past, but there is no sign of it.

You suddenly realise how deathly quiet it is. The howling of the creature has stopped. There is only the mournful sighing of the wind and the distant cries of the Doctor and Martha, as they call your name, wondering where you've gone.

A horrible realisation suddenly dawns on you. Hearing a grunting snort behind you, you turn, eyes wide in horror, and come face to face with the beast. It was already in here waiting for you. There's no getting away from it now. Snarling, the creature seizes you in its terribly taloned hands.

The shock is too much for you and you blackout...

Turn to 75.

Taking the left-hand passageway, you follow it deeper and deeper into the hill. Eventually it comes to a dead-end in front of a huge flat boulder that blocks the tunnel. By the light of the Doctor's hand-held device, you can make out a pattern of combined spiral carvings on its smooth surface.

'Curiouser and curiouser.'

'What is it, Doctor?' Martha ventures.

'I do believe it's a door,' he replies.

'A door?'

'Yes, but don't worry. I have a key,' he says, waggling the device in his hand.

He fiddles with the pen-like object and then points it at the flat boulder. There is a shrill sonic whine and the spiral carving at the stone's centre begins to glow with an inner blue light. You stare, open-mouthed, as with a harsh grating sound the stone slides to one side, revealing another tunnel beyond.

'Sonic screwdriver,' the Doctor grins. 'Never leave home without one.'

You follow as he and Martha advance along the next passageway which soon opens out into a larger circular chamber. You notice that the walls now appear to be made of rough stone, as if cut out of the bedrock beneath Howling Hill. Two more passageways lead away from here.

'Which way now?' Martha asks.

If you want to suggest taking the left-hand tunnel, turn to 61. If you would rather recommend going right, turn to 81.

Sprinting along the tunnel that opens up ahead of you, bumping against the rough-hewn mud and rock walls in the dark, you are startled to see a light suddenly shine from what had been utter blackness ahead of you.

'Ah, that's where you got to,' the Doctor says, lowering his glowing pen-device.

'Are you all right?' Martha asks with genuine concern.

The two of them seem pleased to see you, but not half as pleased as you are to see them. You quickly explain what happened and about your terrifying discovery.

'All sounds very exciting,' says the Doctor enthusiastically. 'I'd like to see that for myself, if that's all right with you?'

Surely the Doctor can't be serious?

If you want to lead the Doctor and Martha back to where you encountered the creature, turn to 101. If you would rather persuade the Doctor to go back the way he just came, turn to 41.

43 The two of you race away as fast as your weary legs will carry you. The chill night air catches in the back of your throat but you push on regardless. You dare not look round, for fear of what you might see. After all, the Doctor's not here to save you this time.

'Over here!' Martha pants, pointing towards the pitch-black entrance to the long barrow. You don't need any more encouragement than that; it's a place to hide, and that's the most you could have hoped for right now.

Ducking your head, you enter the earthwork. A tunnel opens up beyond and you stumble along it, travelling further into the hill after Martha. A few metres further on she stops, gasping for breath. The two of you crouch down behind a half-buried boulder and look back out of the barrow at the small patch of velvet night's sky visible through the narrow entrance.

As you watch, your heart in your mouth, you see an even darker silhouette stride past the entrance. It pauses for a moment, looking around, and you hold your breath, fearful that it might hear your heaving breaths. Then the creature raises its head and howls at the moon. A moment later it is gone.

Turn to 28.

44 'I don't think that's a good idea,' you say as you help Zach to his feet. 'I'm sure the Doctor's got the situation under control. Let's just get out of here, as quickly as we can.'

Zach's movements are clumsy and uncoordinated, as if he's still half-asleep, and so you help him towards the tunnel that leads out of the chamber.

You glance back over your shoulder to see the Doctor and Martha forcing the bronze helmet down on top of the Horror's misshapen skull. It bellows at them and the light in its eyes burns crimson. Then, suddenly, it stops and you fancy you can see sparks crackling around its head.

'Come on,' gasps the Doctor as he and Martha join you and Zach at the entrance to the tunnel. 'It think it's time we all got out of here, don't you?'

Turn to 96.

45 Without waiting to see what it is that would make such an appalling sound, you break into a run, hoping to reach the safety of the cottage as soon as possible.

And there then is someone standing on the path in front of you — a man wearing a trench coat and sneakers, an attractive young woman wearing jeans and a maroon leather jacket at his side. He holds up a pen-like object in front of him, a light shining at its tip. You stumble to a halt in surprise.

With a horrendous roar, something bounds out of the darkness behind you.

'Get down! Quick!' the man shouts. You do as he says: it seems like the sensible choice.

The stranger's curious pen starts emitting a high-pitched sonic whine and the bellowing behind you becomes a pained moaning. You dare to look round and get the impression of lank, green hair, a monstrous misshapen body and glowing-coal eyes, before whatever it is flees into the night again.

'Hello,' says the man, offering you his hand to help you up. 'I'm the Doctor. How do you do?'

If you reply that you have never been so scared in all your life, turn to 91. If you want to ask what he and his companion are doing in Caernbury, at night, turn to 12.

'Umm,' Zach mumbles self-consciously, 'I have a dossier on him.'

'A dossier!' exclaims Martha.

Zach rummages amongst a stack of papers on the caravan's small fold-out table. He pulls out a coffee-stained cardboard folder, and retrieves a hefty wad of documents which are held together with a rubber band, and hands them to Martha.

'I've got all sorts of stuff in there,' he says, as Martha starts to flick through it. 'Copies of police reports concerning the appearance of the Webstar over London on Christmas Day 2006, a patient chart from the Royal Hope Hospital, even a school photograph from Farringham School for Boys in Hertfordshire, dated 1913.'

'You have been busy,' mutters the Doctor, rummaging through some of Zach's other disorganised papers. 'Got a girlfriend, have you? Oh look!' he suddenly exclaims, excitedly holding up a dog-eared copy of the Fortean Times. 'I love this!'

'That's his inner geek speaking,' Martha tells you, with a wink.

'I've appeared in it myself on a number of occasions. Never intentionally, of course.'

With Martha absorbed in the dossier and the Doctor thumbing through the magazine, a great feeling of tiredness suddenly overcoming you, your attention begins to wander — and alights on a curious metal box with its own tiny satellite dish on top.

If you want to ask Zach what it is, turn to 93. If you want to ask him what he's doing here, in the shadow of Howling Hill, turn to 67.

47 'It doesn't look like anything special to me,' Martha says as the Doctor peers at the age-faded markings that were once carved into the surface of the standing stones.

'Well let's see, shall we?'

The Doctor takes out his sonic pen-device and, its blue tip illuminated once more, begins to pass it backwards and forwards across the darkened entrance.

Standing on this blasted hilltop in the face of a biting wind, still only in the clothes you wore to the playing fields, you stamp your feet to ward off the cold as you stand there waiting for the Doctor to finish doing whatever it is he's doing.

If you want to wait patiently for him to finish, turn to 60. If you want to have a look around the site more carefully yourself, turn to 95.

48 You enter the next chamber to see the knotwork patterns carved into the stone walls glowing brilliant white. The light is projecting onto the domed roof of the chamber, looking suspiciously like a star map of the heavens.

'We're running out of time!' gasps the Doctor.

'Why? What does all this mean?' Martha asks, pointing at the map of the Milky Way above you.

'The ship's navigational computer is online again which means it must be preparing for take-off,' he explains. 'But, if that's the case, the ship must think it's got itself a new pilot at long last.'

'This spaceship thinks?' you say. 'But that's imposs—'

'Quick, this way!' the Doctor cuts you off, shouting to be heard over the rising hum that is filling the chamber now.

If you are trying to save Zach Katz, turn to 32. If you have never met Zach Katz, turn to 8.

As you take in the strangely proportioned bones — the compacted ribcage, flattened skull and elongated leg and arm bones — you notice a small, hand-drawn sketch, stuck on the bottom of the display case.

It shows a stone throne, with the curious skeleton seated upon it, the helmet in the other cabinet resting on its bare skull. There's no doubt about it — it is the same throne you found deep beneath the long barrow.

'Definitely alien,' the Doctor says peering over your shoulder.

'That's the throne we found inside the hill!' Martha exclaims gleefully.

'Got it in one,' the Doctor agrees. 'Now, let's take a look at that helmet again, shall we?'

Turn to 19.

50 'Ah yes, the Legend of Howling Hill,' Reverend Stukeley begins. 'It is said that a monster lives inside the hill, in a cave deep below the spot where the long barrow stands. It is said to be a terrible thing, twice as tall as a man and ten times as strong, with teeth like knives and eyes that burn like hot coals. Like Grendel from the Beowulf myth cycle, it steals away people to feed its gruesome appetites.'

'Sounds charming,' the Doctor jumps in. 'I can't wait to meet it.'

The vicar fixes the Doctor with a dark look. 'Well, Professor Smith, you may actually get your chance. It seems that there might be more to the legend than meets the eye in light of this evening's developments. Arthur Cove's excavation certainly never threw up anything like this. At least, I don't think it did. I'll have to visit the local museum again in the morning and take another look at the account in his journal, just to be sure.'

The vicar has given you two potential leads in solving the mystery of the monster that attacked you and that seems to haunt the village of Caernbury.

If you want to ask Reverend Stukeley to tell you more about Arthur Cove and his excavation, turn to 66. If you want to ask him about the village museum, turn to 24.

51 | 'Well, that's the mystery of the legend of Howling Hill put to bed,' the Doctor says, looking pleased with himself.

The four of you are standing in the middle of the village green, in front of a strange blue box that you had never noticed before, whilst gallivanting about with the Doctor.

'No way!' Zach exclaims, unable to contain his excitement.

You can't understand what he's so excited about. 'This is just an old Police call box, isn't it?' you say, bewildered.

'It's a TARDIS,' Martha tells you. 'It just happens to look like an old Police call box.'

'It's the TARDIS actually,' the Doctor points out, 'since it's the only one left.'

'But what is a TARDIS?' you ask.

'It stands for Time and Relative Dimensions in Space,' the Doctor explains.

'I was right!' Zach whoops. 'This is your ship, isn't it?'

'We've got a sharp one here,' the Doctor says, smiling at Martha.

'A spaceship?' you say incredulously.

'That's right,' the Doctor says, pushing open the door. 'Care to take a look inside?'

Peering through the doorway you have your breath taken away as you take in what appears to be a vast control room, impossibly squeezed inside the much smaller Police Box.

'But it's bigger on the inside –' Zach begins.

'Than it is on the outside,' the Doctor finishes for him. 'Yes. I'd sort of noticed that myself. Now then, you two, how about a quick journey? Just one, kind of like a thank you for your help.'

Before you know it, both you and Zach are standing inside the impossible control room with Martha saying, 'That's how it started with me. Just one quick trip.'

And then, with the TARDIS wheezing asthmatically, you're off.

This adventure might be over, but your journey through time and space is only just beginning...

'Magnificent, isn't it?' he says and, before you know it, he's got the cabinet open and is lifting the helmet from its display stand.

Martha looks around nervously, as if she is expecting a burglar alarm to go off. 'Breaking and entering — is there no end to your talents?' she asks him.

'Don't worry,' says the Doctor, realising what she must be thinking. 'I deactivated the alarm before we entered. Now, let's have a look at you, you beauty, shall we?' he says, turning his attention back to the helmet in his hands.

He starts tinkering with the artefact, getting out his sonic screwdriver again.

'That's the telepathic command relays realigned and recalibrated,' he says after a few minutes' fiddling with the helmet. It looks like the Doctor is trying to repair it, although it doesn't actually appear broken to you.

'Nothing very serious,' he goes on, 'but it would have stopped the control helm working as it should. Now, back to the hill, but this time we're taking this with us.'

'Doctor, isn't this stealing?' says Martha warily.

'I think it was Arthur Cove who was the thief, don't you?' the Doctor says sagely. 'We're just going to return this to its original owners, as it were.'

You have never spent such an energetic night as you have this night, running around with the Doctor and Martha. And now you think you can see where it is all leading.

If Zach Katz is with you, turn to 69. If not, turn to 25.

53 The three of you race back through the hill as it shudders and shakes around you. The Doctor opens the stone door for the last time, and then, before you know it, you're sprinting out of the barrow and down the rugged hillside.

A seismic shudder ripples through the ground beneath your feet. A second later, with a deafening roar, half the hillside caves in and something large and black rises from its ages-old resting place beneath Howling Hill. Dripping soil, scrubby vegetation and chunks of chalk, the curious stone ship continues to rise until it is hovering over two hundred feet above you.

It looks not unlike the three-spiral pattern from the stone door beneath the barrow, in that it has three distinct circular parts to it. Then, the engine pods at its rear blazing into life, it rockets away into the night's sky.

The three of you watch the ship depart, until the fire of its engines is nothing more than a speck of light among the millions of stars that cover the vista of the universe beyond the atmosphere of Earth.

'How are you going to explain that, if anyone asks?' Martha asks the Doctor, pointing at the gaping hole in the hillside.

'Oh, I'm sure people will believe it was caused by subsidence.'

'What just happened?' you ask in stunned disbelief.

'You've just been onboard an alien survey ship which crash-landed here thousands of years ago,' the Doctor explain. 'Its pilot was killed in the initial crash — its skeleton is what's in the museum — but the ship was semi-organic and shared a psychic link with its pilot. Without a pilot the ship was unable to take off again. It had been sending out its organic drones — like the Horror that chased you — to find another one ever since. However, the command helm that connected the ship to the pilot was also damaged and so whoever the drones brought back, it never worked and the ship was left trapped here, buried beneath the hill. After Arthur Cove took the helmet from the ship, there wasn't a hope of it ever working. That is, until we returned it to its rightful owner.'

Turn to 102.

While Martha and the Doctor keep their distance you creep up to the caravan, past a chugging, petrol-guzzling generator, and standing on tiptoes, peer in through a grimy window.

You see a young man — probably in his early twenties — tapping away at a keyboard in front of a computer, his wild hair and beard weirdly illuminated by the ghostly glow of the screen.

And then you hear the chilling howl once again and feel a knot of fear form in the pit of your stomach.

'Ooh, that sound,' the Doctor says with a shudder. 'Sets your teeth on edge, doesn't it? Reminds me of that time at the Torchwood Estate in Scotland.'

'When was that?' you ask, happy to be distracted for a moment from the unearthly wailing.

'Oh, let me see. 1879, I think it was.'

'Come on, you two,' urges Martha, 'that thing's still on the loose. What are we going to do now?'

If you want Martha to knock on the door of the caravan now, turn to 88. If you want to hurry back to the village, turn to 2.

Darting suspicious glances about him, the Doctor approaches the locked entrance to the museum. He takes out his curious pen-like device again and touches it to the lock, whilst waggling at the handle.

There is a sudden sharp click and the door opens. 'Voila!' the Doctor says, a delighted grin on his face. 'After you.'

With you leading the way, the three of you file inside. It is very eerie creeping around the darkened museum, the moonlight that manages to make it through the dusty windows alighting on glass display cases and wooden cabinets, their ancient varnish peeling.

Everything is laid out around the walls of what is effectively a single room. There are artefacts from all periods throughout British history including weapons and armour from the English Civil War, and an illuminated medieval manuscript. However, two exhibits attract your interest more than any other.

The first is a skeleton mounted inside a large glass case in the middle of the room. The second is a bronze helmet, the precious stones set into it glittering as they are caught in the moonbeams.

If you want to take a closer look at the skeleton, turn to 9. If you want to study the helmet more closely, turn to 31.

'Look!' Martha calls, pointing over the crest of the hill towards something far below.

There, parked in the corner of a field at the bottom of the hill, is a grubby white caravan. You are surprised to see a satellite dish sitting on its roof, which reflects the light of the moon from its gleaming surface.

'What do you make of that?'

'It's a caravan with a satellite dish on the roof.' The Doctor can't help but sound intrigued himself.

'But what's it doing here?'

'That's a good question,' he replies. 'Unfortunately, it's not one we've really got time to try and answer now.'

'What do you mean?' Martha asks, surprised.

'We're not done here yet and if we're to solve the mystery of the Horror of Howling Hill once and for all, I feel we need to head back to the village post haste.'

'I bet there's a connection,' Martha persists.

'Well,' says the Doctor, 'you could be right.' He turns to you. 'What's it to be? The village or the caravan?'

If you want to head back to Caernbury as the Doctor suggests, turn to 2. If you want to go with Martha's idea of visiting the caravan, turn to 27.

57 Three things hit you when you enter the circular chamber, which contains a strangely out-of-place standing stone at its centre. One, the stone is glowing brightly, two, a rising, throbbing hum is reverberating from the walls, and three, the whole place is shaking as if caught in an earthquake.

'The power source has been activated,' the Doctor says, uneasily.

'That's just what we need,' says Martha anxiously, as she stares at the glowing stone.

'This ship is preparing for lift-off, which must mean that it thinks it's got itself a new pilot,' the Doctor continues.

'Thinks?' you say in disbelief.

'Come on, this way!' he orders, heading for the other tunnel leading out of this chamber.

If you are trying to save Zach Katz, turn to 32. If you have never met Zach Katz, turn to 8.

Your heart pounding in your chest, you race for home, hearing the horrid creature bounding after you along the path.

Suddenly you hear a young woman's voice shout from nearby: 'Over here, Doctor! Someone's in trouble!'

A moment later, a high-pitched sonic whine pierces the night. The monster cries out behind you again, only this time it sounds like it's in pain.

'Ah, so that's where it got to.' This time the voice belongs to a man, a man who emerges from the darkness in front of you. He is wearing a trench coat and sneakers and at his side is a pretty young woman in her twenties wearing jeans and a maroon leather jacket. In one outstretched hand is a pen-like object which emits a bright blue light from its tip. It is this device which is making the whining sound.

With one last feral scream, the pursuing monster vanishes back into the enveloping night. You stumble to a halt in stunned surprise.

'Hello,' says the man warmly, putting away the curious, now silent, device and offering you his hand. 'I'm the Doctor. How do you do?'

If you reply that you have never been so scared in all your life, turn to 91. If you simply want to ask what he and his companion are doing in Caernbury at night, turn to 12.

'I thought we'd done that one,' says the man, looking at you with something like kindly curiosity. 'I'm the Doctor and this is Miss Martha Jones, my travelling companion.'

'Pleased to meet you,' says the young woman. 'Look, are you okay? Only you've had a nasty scare.'

Although you feel shaken by your experience you feel excited as well and tell Martha that you're all right.

'Right, good,' says the Doctor. 'Let's be on our way then. We've still got a monster to catch, you know, Martha?'

Turn to 63.

'You'd be mistaken to say that this doesn't look like anything special,' the Doctor says. 'I'm picking up a trace energy signal from inside the hill.'

'I stand corrected,' his companion says, pulling her leather jacket even tighter about her against the chill bite of the wind. The Doctor doesn't seem to be bothered by the cold.

Just then another chilling cry echoes across the windswept hilltop. There can be no mistaking the bestial howl that cuts through the chill night air. The monster has caught up with you again. The hunters have suddenly become the hunted.

'Come on,' the Doctor says, his tone urgent. 'In here.'

The three of you duck inside the barrow to find a tunnel leading away from you into the hillside. It smells of damp earth and crumbling chalk. Following the passageway, the Doctor leading the way, you come at last to a T-junction.

'Hmm, which way now, I wonder?' The Doctor holds up his sonic scanner again.

If you want to suggest he takes the left-hand passage, turn to 41. If you want to go right, turn to 101.

61 Exiting via this passageway, you come out in a second circular chamber. The walls are faced with cut stones which have been carved with yet more knotwork patterns, like those favoured by the Celts, and the same repeating spiral pattern you saw on the stone door.

'I can honestly say I have never seen anything quite like this,' the Doctor says in wonder, his voice echoing back to you by the weird acoustics of the underground chamber.

Another circular tunnel leads onwards into the hill on the other side of the chamber.

If you think you should push on, turn to 38. If you want to stay here a while and have a closer look at the intricate carvings, turn to 21.

You sprint between the trees, hearing the monster crashing through the branches behind you a split second later. And then the unthinkable happens.

Your foot catches against an exposed tree root and you are sent flying into the musty leaf mould that covers the ground.

You flip yourself round, onto your back, in time to see the hideous creature bearing down on your, gangly arms outstretched, lips pulled back and teeth bared in a feral snarl.

Then the Doctor is there once more, the sonic screwdriver gripped in his hand emitting its shrill sonic whine. The monster howls and backs away, dropping the helmet as it throws its misshapen hands over its ears. Still holding the sonic emitter out in front of him, the Doctor quickly recovers the bronze helmet.

However, it doesn't flee as it did the first time you encountered it. Now that the Doctor has the helmet, the Grendel-beast seems more reluctant to let you get away, despite the obvious pain it is suffering under the influence of the screwdriver.

'Come on!' shouts the Doctor, as you scramble to your feet to join him and Martha once again. 'I don't know how long I can hold off that thing anymore.'

Turn to 89.

'Wait!' you hear yourself say. 'Let me come with you.'

The Doctor fixes you with those penetrating eyes of his. 'Hmm, I'm not so sure. I mean, I don't like the idea of putting you in danger.'

'But surely three of us looking would be better than two,' you say, 'and you've probably lost its trail thanks to me. Let me help you and I'm sure we'll be able to track it down again in no time.'

A frown of consternation creases the Doctor's brow and he sucks in his top lip as he looks you up and down.

'Our young friend's got a point,' Martha says, speaking up for you, 'and you did say there's nothing to worry about.'

'Did I?'

'Well, as good as.'

Silence descends between the two of them, leaving you shooting anxious glances at this mysterious Doctor and his companion.

'Oh, go on then,' the Doctor says, 'if you think you're up to it.'

'I am!' you assert, excitedly.

'Very well then,' the Doctor smiles, mischievously, 'which way do you think the creature went?'

Peering through the encroaching night you can't exactly miss the massive black shape of Howling Hill. But nearby you can also see the silhouette of a church tower, stark against the backdrop of the night's sky.

Then you hear the creature's dread howl again, but which direction did it come from?

If you want to head towards the village church, turn to 10. If you want to direct the others towards the hill itself, turn to 100.

64 It is a brave thing you do, turning to face the beast, but in the end it is also a futile act of courage. Face to face with the creature you realise that you could never hope to overcome something that is seven feet of corded muscle guided by a relentless animal intelligence.

Snarling, the creature seizes you in its terribly taloned hands. The shock is too much for you and, with a feeble cry, you collapse in a dead faint...

Turn to 75.

65 'No, leave me here!' Zach shouts as the three of you haul him from the throne. 'It's what I want! I promise you!'

As he struggles against you all, the helmet falls from his head onto the stone seat.

'This is no time for misplaced heroics!' the Doctor tells him firmly. 'We're not leaving you behind!'

Turn to 96.

'Arthur Cove was the archaeologist who excavated the barrow a hundred years ago, in 1908,' Reverend Stukeley explains. 'He supposedly found a tunnel leading into the hill wherein he found the treasure of some long dead Celtic king. Cove brought some of the treasures he found there back with him.'

'Really?' exclaims the Doctor, intrigued. 'Where are these treasures now?'

'Why, they form the main exhibit at the village museum, of course,' the vicar replies. 'Has your research not taken you there yet?'

'Thank you for your help, Reverend Stukeley,' the Doctor says suddenly, leaping into action, 'but it's time we were on our way.' He gives you a conspiratorial wink.

When the three of you are standing outside the church in the lane again Martha asks, 'Where now, Doctor?'

Folding his arms, the Doctor raises one eyebrow and, grinning at you says, 'Why don't we let our young friend here decide.'

If you think you should all head for hill, turn to 100. If you want to visit the village museum, turn to 3.

67 'Investigating the Legend of Howling Hill, of course.'

'Of course,' the Doctor humours him.

'There's something funny going on here, I tell you. Like that place, Fetch Priory, back in the 70s,' Zach goes on. 'There's a conspiracy of silence surrounding the disappearances that have occurred around here.'

'You really think so?' Martha says, challenging his wild conspiracy theorist claim.

'Oh yes. It's been going on for years — centuries in fact.'

Considering your own close shave at the hands of the hunting monster, you are keen to know what Zach's research has thrown up.

To ask him what he thinks is behind the legend, turn to 34. To ask him why he thinks the attacks are happening again now, turn to 4.

It is as you are cautiously backing away from the creature — your heart racing as it pumps adrenalin around you body in case you suddenly need to run from danger — that you realise something is wrong with the creature.

It hasn't tried to attack you once and for a creature that seems to spend most of its time howling, it is surprisingly silent. And there's something else: rather than blazing with inner fire, its eyes are lifeless hollows.

Incredible as it might seem, it would appear that the creature is either paralysed or... dead!

'Ah, there you are,' comes the Doctor's voice from behind you. Martha is with him.

'Are you all right?' she asks.

They both seem pleased to see you, but not half as pleased as you are to see them. You quickly explain what happened but the Doctor seems more interested in the monster standing stock-still at the end of the passageway.

Turn to 6.

Hurrying along the darkened country lanes, your way ahead bathed in cold moonlight, you head back towards the looming presence of Howling Hill.

Your route takes you passed the field in which Zach's caravan is parked. As you get close he suddenly pipes up, 'Can you just wait a second?'

'What on Earth for?' asks the Doctor, stumbling to a halt.

'I just want to get my digital camera, to record this moment for posterity,' Zach explains. 'Then I can email Keith the pictures. He's never going to believe this!'

'I'm not sure now's really the time,' the Doctor says warily, 'and time is, as always, of the essence.'

If you want to tell Zach to forget the camera and come with you, turn to 99. If you don't say anything, turn to 84.

The three of you race back through the hill as it shudders and shakes around you. The Doctor opens the stone door for the last time, and in no time you're sprinting out of the barrow and down the rugged hillside.

A dull boom rumbles through the ground beneath your feet and echoes across the landscape for miles around. A second later you hear a deafening crump as half the hillside collapses in on itself.

When the dust has settled and the retort of the ship's exploding engines has faded into silence once more, the three of you stagger to your feet and survey the damage.

'How are you going to explain that, if anyone asks?' Martha challenges the Doctor, pointing at the newly gaping hole in the hillside.

'Oh, I'm sure people will just put it down to subsidence,' he says.

'What just happened?' you ask in stunned disbelief.

'Haven't you worked it out yet?' the Doctor laughs. 'You were trapped onboard an alien survey ship which crash-landed here thousands of years ago. Its pilot was killed in the initial crash but the ship was semi-organic and shared a psychic link with its pilot. Without a pilot the ship was unable to take off again. It's been sending out its organic drones

— the Horrors — to find another one ever since. However, the command helm that connects the ship to the pilot was damaged and so whoever the drones brought back, it never worked and so the ship was still stuck here. And after Arthur Cove took it from the ship, there wasn't a hope of it ever working.'

Turn to 102.

As Martha takes off towards the barrow's entrance, you leg it away from this spot as well, even as you see the monster lolloping out of the darkness between the trees of the knotted wood towards you.

There is no one to help you now and few places to hide.

If you want to run after Martha towards the entrance of the barrow, turn to 17. If you would rather try to wrong-foot the charging creature by making for the rear of the large mound, turn to 95.

There are artefacts on display from all periods of British history. They range from weapons and armour from the English Civil War to an illuminated medieval manuscript. However, there are two exhibits which attract your attention more than any other.

The first is a skeleton mounted inside a large glass case in the middle of the room. Martha is studying this one with great fascination. The Doctor is more intrigued by the second exhibit — a bronze helmet, the precious stones set into it glittering as they are caught in the moonbeams.

If you want to look at the skeleton, with Martha, turn to 37. If you want to join the Doctor in studying the helmet, turn to 52.

73 Bravely you run after the Grendel-monster, coming right up behind it as it continues to bear down on the Doctor.

'Quick, Doctor!' you shout, with a moment's flash of inspiration. 'Throw me the helmet!'

Eyes narrowed, as if he is wondering what you have in mind, the Doctor does as you request and tosses you the helmet. You catch it deftly in one hand and, before the creature even has time to turn around, you leap up and ram it down firmly on top of its head.

The Horror bellows again and turns on you, the light in its eyes burning crimson. Oh no, what have you done?

Suddenly it stops and you see sparks crackling around the helmet as well as the beast's misshapen skull.

'Come on,' gasps the Doctor. 'I think it's time we all got out of here, don't you?'

As the two of you run for the exit, you see Martha helping Zach up from the throne. His movements appear clumsy and uncoordinated, as if he's half-asleep. And then, all reunited at the tunnel entrance once more, you flee the throne room.

Turn to 96.

'I've made my assessment,' the Doctor announces, his voice echoing hollowly from the cavern walls. He looks at you expectantly, as if waiting for you to say something.

'And what are your conclusions?' Martha asks, providing him with his cue.

'We're inside a spaceship,' he says, beaming.

'I'd guessed that much.'

'How could you know that?' you ask in amazement.

'Occupational hazard of travelling with the Doctor,' she confides, smiling now as well.

You feel completely overwhelmed. 'What is it you do, Doctor?' you find yourself asking, as you try to make sense of everything you've experienced over the last few hours since you first met the Doctor and Martha.

'We are travellers,' the Doctor says, suddenly serious, 'in time and space. We're inside an alien spaceship that probably crashed here thousands of years ago, and the monster that's been chasing you is some kind of organic robot. Will that do for an explanation?'

Dumbfounded, you say nothing.

'Right then,' he says, clapping his hands together, 'I'm glad we've got that sorted out. Now, if we're going to solve this mystery once and for all I think we're going to need to get back to the village. Allons-y!'

Following the Doctor, who sets off at an energetic pace, you trudge back through what he claims to be a buried spaceship, finally exited it again through the long barrow at the top of the hill.

If you touched something while you were exploring the tunnels beneath the barrow, which had an unexpected effect, turn to 13. If not, turn to 56.

You come to in darkness. Then, as you slowly open your eyes, a dull blue light begins to permeate the vaulted chamber in which you find yourself, and you become aware of a dull humming sound.

You are seated upon the cold stone throne at the heart of Howling Hill. It is then that you realise that the helmet from the museum has been placed on your head. It feels warm against your scalp.

As the light in the chamber brightens you gasp, seeing the monster again in front of you. But now it is motionless, standing still as a statue against the wall of the domed vault, the light in its eyes pulsing in time with the light coming from the dressed stone wall of the chamber.

A throbbing vibration passes through the throne and into you. If what you now find yourself inside is in fact a spaceship, then you could well believe that it is powering up, ready for take off.

If you want to take the helmet off with further ado, turn to 16. If you want to stay precisely where you are, turn to 92.

76 You enter the small church of St Nicholas, wincing at the brightness of the light inside, after the all-consuming darkness of the night outside. The air is thick with the smell of dusty hymnals and candle wax. It also appears to be empty.

'Will you look at that?' Martha gasps, staring in amazement at the window above the altar, her fear of churches having apparently evaporated.

'Remarkable,' the Doctor says, putting on a pair of dark-rimmed spectacles, as though to study the window more closely. 'I tell you, the human race, remarkable.'

What does he mean the human race? Isn't he part of it?

You look more closely too, and what you see certainly isn't what you would have expected inside a church. The painted leaded panes show an image of what you take to be the village, nestled beneath the hill, only in the sky above the hill is what is quite clearly supposed to be a falling star, or comet, its fiery tail blazing after it.

You almost jump out of your skin when the church door slams shut, the boom echoing back from the bare plastered walls and a grim voice demands, 'Can I help you?'

Turn to 15.

77 The three of you press on up the escarpment, your leg muscles burning with the effort of climbing the rugged hillside for the second time in one night.

The Doctor is almost at the summit when a terrifying figure looms out of the darkness at the top of the hill and gives voice to a hideous howl. Arms outstretched above it, green hair hanging in lank, matted folds, the Horror lashes out with one horribly taloned claw of a hand, and catches the Doctor across the face.

Martha screams as the Doctor is sent flying sideways, the helmet knocked out of his hands. The monster begins to bear down on him. With the Doctor out of action, what are you going to do?

If you want to run from the beast, turn to 33. If you want to grab the helmet before the creature can, turn to 94.

The Doctor looks at you, eyes narrowing.

'Are you sure?' he says solemnly.

'He said it's what he wants,' you reply, 'to see beyond the stars.'

The Doctor looks back at the prone Zach and then at the screen with its scrolling alien script.

'I can understand that. Very well then. Farewell, Zachary, and bon voyage.' He turns back to you and Martha. 'It's time we were going, or this thing is going to take off with us still onboard too!'

Turn to 53.

| '**H**ELP!' you scream. 'Anyone? Help me!'

The monster stays exactly where it is, still watching you intently with those glowing-coal eyes. And then it makes its move.

Even as the creature lunges for you, you hear a high-pitched sonic whine and the monster throws its misshapen hands over its ears. It howls again, although now it sounds like it's in pain.

'Ah, that's where it's got to,' comes a sprightly male voice from somewhere else nearby.

Taking your eyes off the monster for a moment, you glance to your left to see a man approaching you out of the darkness. He appears to be in his thirties, and is wearing a brown trench coat and sneakers. He is holding a pen-like object out in front of him, a blue light shining at its tip. Beside him is a pretty girl in her twenties, wearing jeans and a maroon leather jacket.

With one last feral scream, the ungainly monster turns tail and vanishes into the enveloping night. Stunned, you stay where you are, trying to take in all that has happened to you in the last few minutes.

'Hello,' says the man warmly, putting away the curious, now silent, device and offering you his hand. 'I'm the Doctor. How do you do?'

Will you reply that you have never been so scared in all your life, by turning to 91. Or will you simply ask him what he and his companion are doing here, in Caernbury, at night, by turning to 12?

80 In no time at all, the Doctor has let you all into the museum for a second time. The helmet and skeleton remain on display where they have done, undisturbed, for the last hundred years.

But now you see them with new eyes. Knowing that they were discovered beneath Howling Hill and having been there for yourself since your last visit to the museum, you realise that these two finds are more significant than at first any of you realised.

Somehow you know that they hold the key to stopping the Horror of Howling Hill once and for all.

To take a look at the strange skeleton, turn to 49. To look at the helmet, turn to 19.

81 You enter another circular domed chamber, almost identical to the last, except for the lone standing stone at its centre. In the torch-beam of the Doctor's sonic screwdriver, it appears to glitter with quartz crystals — or something very much like them — embedded in its surface.

'Now why would someone go to all the bother of erecting a standing stone down here?' the Doctor asks, although you suspect that he isn't expecting an answer.

You are drawn to the curious quartz-light which casts skittering patterns of light onto the dressed stone walls of the chamber.

If you want to reach out and touch the stone, turn to 14. If you would rather lead the way out of this chamber into the next one, turn to 38.

82 | Running over to the throne, you shake Zach by the shoulders, calling his name, desperately trying to rouse him.

Slowly he opens his eyes. 'Wh-What's going on?' he mumbles.

'The Doctor's under attack!' you exclaim. 'We've got to get you out of here. We're here to save you!'

'It looks like the Doctor's the one who needs saving,' he says, suddenly seeming more alert. 'But it's okay, I know what to do. Give me the helmet.'

If you want to get the helmet for Zach, turn to 23. If you just want to get him out of harm's way as quickly as possible, turn to 44.

'I heard it first on my way home from the park,' you explain. 'It scared me half to death.'

'I'm not surprised,' the Reverend Stukeley admits. 'But wait a minute, I thought, Professor, you said that this was one of your students.'

'Yes,' the Doctor bluffs, 'one of my students, who I bumped into again on the path from the park.'

'Well, you'd best be on your way and get off home,' the vicar says, addressing you again. 'I'm sure the Professor will see you home safely. After all, we don't want any more disappearances, do we?'

Disappearances? What disappearances?

If you want to ask the Reverend Stukeley more about these disappearances, turn to 22. If you would rather be on your way, as he suggests, and head now for the hill instead, turn to 100.

Zach hops back over the stile into the field while the rest of you press on for the hill. Only a matter of moments later you hear a nerve-shredding howl, which is followed by a petrified scream and a terrible rending sound.

'Zach!' Martha calls out, but her cry is met by a silence more chilling than the scream that preceded it.

'Come on!' the Doctor shouts to you both, running for the stile himself now. 'He needs our help.'

Turning on your heels, you and Martha both chase after the Doctor, heading back towards the caravan.

When you enter the field you are met by a scene of utter devastation. The caravan has been torn open as if it were made of paper. Zach's carefully collected documents are strewn across the muddy ruts of the field or caught in the hedgerows. You see his computer lying smashed on the floor of the ripped open caravan, but of Zach himself there is no sign.

'Oh, Doctor,' Martha says, appalled. 'What have we done?'

'He's been abducted. The creature must have taken him,' the Doctor says darkly. 'If we're going to help him we have to get back to that barrow!'

Turn to 99.

Hearing a mournful moaning sound you jump, expecting the monster that was hunting you earlier to leap out of the darkness at you. But when no such attack comes, you realise that the sound you heard was nothing more than the wind sighing through the branches of the trees.

Then you hear a cry and this time you know that something is wrong. 'Doctor?' you hear Martha shouting. 'Doctor!'

You sprint back between the trees to the long barrow. Martha is standing there alone, hugging her leather jacket tight to herself, frantically pacing up and down over the wind-rippled grass.

'He was here one minute and gone the next!' she exclaims. 'It's like he's disappeared into thin air!'

In the stunned silence with which you greet Martha's words, a second chilling cry rings out across the barren blasted hilltop. This time there's no mistaking the bestial sound. The monster has found you.

'Quick! Run!' Martha screams.

If you think that the best way to escape from the monster is for the two of you to split up, turn to 71. If you think it is a better idea to stick with Martha, turn to 43.

'Well, if that's what we're going to do, everyone keep quiet,' hisses the Doctor.

In the silence you become uncomfortably aware of how loud your breathing is, so you hold your breath. But your heart is still beating its drum-roll of fear, playing your ribcage like a xylophone. You can't believe that the monster can't hear it, it's so loud.

But, faced with the chance of finding an answer to the mystery that has become his obsession, Zach can contain himself no longer. Grabbing a small digital camera from the table he flings open the door and runs out into the night.

The Doctor is about to chase after him when you all hear that terrible roar again and a terrified scream, followed by an ominous silence.

'He's been taken,' the Doctor states, his face a dark grimace.

'Shouldn't we do something?' Martha exclaims, joining him at the door.

'Yes, we should, but we can't do anything for him here. The best thing we can do to help Zach now it to solve this mystery ourselves. Quick, follow me, back to the village!'

The Doctor leading the way, you leave the caravan, dash across the field, scramble over a stile and race off along a country lane, back towards the village. The Doctor holds his sonic screwdriver out in front of him, as if scanning for something. And so, you come at last to Caernbury's archaeological museum.

If you have already visited the village museum, turn to 80. If you haven't been there before, turn to 2.

87 With the monster bearing down on you, the distance between you and it decreasing dramatically with every bounding step, you are going to have to act fast if you are to get away.

In desperation you scan the hilltop for somewhere to hide. Only two places seem suitable; the coppice of twisted, wind-blown trees and the long barrow itself.

If you want to head into the wood, turn to 62. If you want to make for the barrow, turn to 40.

A grungy young man answers the door. His orange hair is matted into dreadlocks and he has a wispy ginger beard on his pasty white chin. He is wearing a coarse poncho that would be described elsewhere as 'ethnic' and baggy tie-dyed trousers.

'Yes? Can I help you?' he asks rather testily on seeing Martha.

'Um, yes, well,' she struggles to begin.

'Oh my goodness, it's you!' the man suddenly exclaims, looking past Martha at the Doctor standing behind her, his prized sneakers plastered with mud.

'It was last time I looked,' he says uncertainly.

'This is unreal! Those saddos on FaceSpace are never going to believe this! I never thought I'd actually get to meet you, in person and everything. Wait till I tell Keith — he's going to be so jealous!'

'Who's Keith?' Martha whispers, so that only you and the Doctor can hear.

'I have no idea,' the Doctor hisses back.

'But where are my manners?' the young man says, suddenly remembering himself. 'Come in, come in.'

The three of you squeeze into the cramped caravan after the excited young Doctor-spotter. You had no idea there were others who already knew of this man you have found yourself with on an adventure.

The caravan itself is something else. It is full of what looks to you like junk, mixed in with a fair amount of computer equipment — towers, monitors, scanners and other assorted electrical gubbins. It also smells rather musty, like unwashed socks, which is also what the bearded geek smells like.

'Look, don't think me rude,' says Martha, 'but who are you?'

'Sorry, sorry, should have said.' Ignoring both you and Martha he wipes his sweaty palm on his trousers and then holds it out to the Doctor. 'Zach Katz at your service. Pleased to meet you, Doctor.'

You can't help but be intrigued.

If you want to ask Zach how he knows about the Doctor, turn to 46. If you want to ask him what he's doing here, turn to 67.

'Quick, into the barrow!' the Doctor urges.

Without needing any further encouragement, the three of you hurry inside, racing along the tunnel until you come to the strange stone door again. At the press of a switch on the Doctor's trusty sonic screwdriver, the door slides open again and you enter what he claims is the spaceship once more.

Reaching the circular chamber with two exits, which way will you lead Martha and the Doctor on the way to the throne room?

If you go left, turn to 48. If you go right, turn to 57.

90 'It's seventeenth century, you know,' the Reverend Stukeley explains, 'but the scene it depicts comes from a legend which dates much further back than that.'

'Really?' says the Doctor. 'How fascinating.'

'Oh yes. It certainly pre-dates the Roman invasion of Britain and possibly goes back as far as the Bronze Age.'

'You're kidding me!' Martha exclaims.

'No, young lady, I can assure you that I am not kidding you, as you put it,' the vicar says, the gleam of scholarly excitement in his eye. 'The story of the star that fell to earth here at Caernbury and the Legend of Howling Hill appear to be linked, along with the disappearances.'

Disappearances? What disappearances?

If you want to ask the Reverend Stukeley more about these disappearances, turn to 22. If you would rather ask him to tell you more about the Legend of Howling Hill, turn to 50.

'Oh, that wasn't scary. Not really,' says the man, grinning wickedly. 'Not when you've been toe-to-toe with the Sycorax or battled the Cybermen.'

'Or the Carrionites,' the young woman throws in. 'Now they were scary!'

'Yes, good point,' says the man. 'I can see where you're coming from there.'

Who are these people and what are they talking about?

Your mind is suddenly full of questions, but which ones do you want answers to?

If you want to ask the two strangers what they are doing in Caernbury at night, go to 12. If you simply want to ask them who they are, turn to 59.

The rising humming reverberating throughout the chamber increases. At the same time, a screen of light appears in the air in front of the throne. Strange blue patterns — not unlike the knotwork carvings that you have seen within the barrow, covering every dressed stone surface — flicker across the screen. Somehow you know that this is some alien script.

Your head throbs with the pulsing sound, inexplicable images filling your mind's eye, and you realise what happened here, all those thousands of years ago, and what is happening now.

A shout breaks through the alien voice speaking in your head, ruining your concentration, and then the helmet is being lifted from your head.

Shaking your head, as you come to your senses, as if waking from a dream, you see the Doctor in front of you, holding the helmet in his hands, and Martha watching you with obvious concern.

'Come on,' he shouts, to be heard over the throbbing hum. 'We haven't got much time before the crystal-matrix core engines overload and this whole place blows.'

If you want to do as the Doctor says and run for it, turn to 70. If you try to persuade him to do something to save the spaceship, turn to 36.

93 Before the young man can answer, the Doctor chips in saying, 'My, my. That's a primitive modulating energy pulse wave detection unit, if I'm not very much mistaken.'

'It's a scanner,' Zach corrects him.

'That's what I said, wasn't it?' replies the Doctor, sounding hurt.

'I made it myself.'

'Very clever,' the Doctor concedes. 'And what have you been scanning with it?'

'The hill, and, believe it or not, it's started picking up a weak energy signal, like a repeating energy pulse.'

'Oh I believe it,' the Doctor grins.

He is about to say something else when that now oh-so familiar dread howl shatters the eerie still of the night.

94 You snatch the helmet from literally right under the monster's grotesque snout of a nose. Drawing on reserves of energy you didn't know you had, from somewhere deep within, you sprint off up the hill, the precious artefact cradled in your arms.

Then you hear the familiar, comforting whine of the Doctor's sonic screwdriver and the monster howls again. Only now that you have the helmet — something which really belongs inside the throne chamber beneath the hill — the creature seems more determined than ever not to let you get away.

'Don't stop!' Martha gasps at your shoulder. 'Just keep moving.'

'Hopefully that should hold it off long enough for us to get a head start,' the Doctor says, appearing at your other side.

Turn to 89.

In the darkness you don't see the rabbit hole. As you round the end of the barrow mound, your foot slips from under you and you suddenly find yourself sliding down a muddy chute in the ground. This is no mere rabbit hole!

Having carried you several metres down into the earth, the curious rabbit hole deposits you inside a more spacious tunnel underground. You pick yourself up and brush yourself down, waiting as your eyesight becomes accustomed to the gloom. A little light from the moon reaches down the shaft into the hill enabling you to make out your surroundings a little better.

And there, looming in front of you is the beast, its lank green hair hanging from its gangly limbs in a matted mess, its eyes black pits in the darkness.

How are you going to react to this latest development?

If you want to run for it, turn to 42. If you want to slowly back away from the creature, turn to 68.

The four of you hurry back through the passageways and chambers of the ship until you reach the strange stone door again. The Doctor opens it and then in no time at all you're sprinting out of the barrow and down the rugged hillside, the ground shuddering violently beneath your feet.

A dull boom ripples through the escarpment throwing you all to the ground. The aftershock of the explosion echoes across the landscape for miles around. A second later you hear a crashing roar as half the hillside collapses in on itself.

When the dust and dirt has settled, the Doctor, Martha, Zach and yourself clamber to your feet and take in the devastation that the destruction of the ship has caused. There is now a gaping crater in one side of Howling Hill.

'How are we supposed to explain that?' Zach asks, staring in amazement at the vast hole in the ground.

'Oh, I'm sure people will just put it down to subsidence,' the Doctor says casually.

'What just happened?' you ask in disbelief.

'Haven't you worked it out yet?' the Doctor laughs. 'That was an alien survey ship buried under there. It must have crash-landed here thousands of years ago. Its pilot was killed but, being semi-organic, the ship shared a psychic link with its pilot and so without one it was unable to take off again.

It's been sending out its organic drones — like the Horror that chased you — to find another one ever since. However, the command helm that connected the ship to the pilot was damaged and so whoever the drones brought back, it never worked, leaving the ship still stuck here. And after Arthur Cove took the helmet from the ship, there wasn't a hope of it ever working.'

Turn to 51.

97 'And what did Arthur Cove's dig uncover?' the Doctor asks, testing the depth of the young man's research.

'A magnificent Bronze Age helmet and a curious skeleton that was dubbed Caernbury Man. But I've seen it and it doesn't look like any kind of human being to me.'

The Doctor fixes Zach with that penetrating stare of his. 'What does it look like to you?'

Without any hesitation Zach declares, 'It looks alien, to me.'

In the silence that follows Zach's revelation, a horribly familiar howl cuts through the still of the night beyond the caravan.

Turn to 30.

'Who are you, and what are you doing in my graveyard?' comes a stern voice from out of the darkness ahead of you.

You watch in open-mouthed surprise as a short, round-faced man appears from behind a moss-covered cross. He is caught for a moment in the moonlight and you see, quite clearly, the stark white dog collar at his neck

'Professor Smith,' the Doctor says, taking a step towards the vicar and holding out his hand. 'Professor John Smith, from the institute. Can I help you, Reverend…?'

'Stukeley,' the vicar replies. 'I heard a noise, a terrible wailing sound, and came out here to investigate,' he goes on. 'A horrible howling it was, like something out of the legend.'

A couple of things the Reverend Stukeley has said intrigue you. Standing next to the Doctor you could suggest a question for him to ask to find out more.

If you want to ask about the howling the vicar heard, turn to 35. If you want to ask about the legend he mentioned, turn to 50.

99 And so, at last, out of breath, but a rush of adrenalin giving you a second wind, you find yourself back at the summit of Howling Hill.

'Where now?' Zach asks, looking around him.

'Where now, he says,' the Doctor laughs. 'Why, into the hill, of course!'

The four of you hurry inside, racing along the tunnel beyond until you come to the strange stone door again. At the press of a switch on the Doctor's trusty sonic screwdriver, the door slides open again and you enter what he claims is the spaceship once more.

With a terrible roar, the Grendel-beast launches itself out of the darkness of the tunnel ahead of you. It has been lying in wait for you here. With one great swipe of a taloned arm it floors the Doctor, and before either you or Martha can do anything to stop it, the creature seizes Zach in its monstrous hands.

It lifts him bodily off the ground as he shouts, kicks and struggles against it — but all to no avail. In moments it is gone, disappearing back into the darkness. You are torn as to who to help first but, seeing Martha's concern at the Doctor's plight, you join her at his side.

'Doctor, are you all right?' she asks, gently shaking him by the shoulder.

The Doctor sits up suddenly, startling both of you.

'Never felt better!' he announces. 'Although I'm not sure the same could be said of Zach. We'd better get after him. There's no time to lose. Allons-y!'

Racing further into the hill, after the monster and Zach, you come to the circular chamber with two exits again.

To go left, turn to 48. To go right, turn to 57.

Without further delay, the three of you set off for the hill. It takes nearly an hour to scale the rugged escarpment. The bitter night air whips around you on this exposed tor.

The Doctor is staring intently in the direction of the barrow. To you it looks like nothing more than a long grassy mound with a narrow entrance at one end between two large standing stones.

'Now what's so special about this place, I wonder,' the Doctor muses. 'It's got the feel of that place on the Novrosk Peninsula in northern Russia.'

'Nov-what?' Martha interrupts. 'Is this just another one of those trips down memory lane for you?'

'There's more here than meets the eye,' the Doctor announces and begins pacing out the perimeter of the ancient earthwork. Martha jogs to catch up with him.

If you want to investigate the barrow with the Doctor and Martha, turn to 47. If you want to explore the small wood beyond it while they're busy instead, turn to 85.

Standing at the end of the passageway is the horror you had hoped never to see again. Looming over you all is the monster, seven-feet tall, three hundred pounds of corded muscle, clawing limbs and cruel fangs. But that's all it's doing, looming.

Something's not right. The creature is silent and hasn't attempted to attack you once. And there's something else — its eyes are lifeless hollows. No smouldering light burns there now.

Turn to 6.

'**W**ell, that's the mystery of the legend of Howling Hill put to bed,' the Doctor says, looking pleased with himself.

The three of you are standing on Caernbury village green, in front of a strange blue box. The sign above the door reads: Police Box. However, Martha tells you that it is really the Doctor's own spaceship; something called a TARDIS.

'Goodbye,' says the Doctor jovially, shaking you warmly by the hand. 'Thank you for all you've done. If we ever need your help, can we call on you again?'

You can't believe what you're hearing. 'Yes, of course!' you exclaim excitedly, without hesitation.

'Take care,' Martha says, ruffling your hair, 'and good luck.'

Then the wooden blue door shuts and, with an asthmatic wheeze the TARDIS fades out of existence before your eyes. You are alone once more as the coming sunrise paints the sky salmon pink.

Buzzing from the thrill of your adventure with Martha and the Doctor, you turn back towards the holiday cottage. Part of you wonders how you are going to explain why your bed hasn't been slept in all night. But another part of you is too busy to worry, wondering when you and the Doctor will meet again.

THE END

Step into a world of wonder and mystery with Sarah Jane and her gang in:

1. Invasion of the Bane
2. Revenge of the Slitheen
3. Eye of the Gorgon
4. Warriors of the Kudlak

And don't miss these other exciting adventures with the Doctor!

1. The Spaceship Graveyard
2. Alien Arena
3. The Time Crocodile
4. The Corinthian Project
5. The Crystal Snare
6. War of the Robots
7. Dark Planet
8. The Haunted Wagon Train
9. Lost Luggage
10. Second Skin
11. The Dragon King
12. The Horror of Howling Hill